Measure for Measure

by Mike Graf and Kathleen McFarren

Measure for Measure

Text: Mike Graf and Kathleen McFarren
Design: Rana Biner
Cover design: Karen Mayo
Editor: Anne McKenna
Illustrations: Boris Silvestri
Typeset in Plantin

Acknowledgements
Photographs by Australian Picture Library/ Corbis/ AFP, p. 10 top/ Adrian Carroll, p. 21/ Chris Golley, p. 30/ Nick Hawkes, p. 29/ George H. H. Huey, p. 17/ Araldo de Luca, p. 23 left/ Paul A. Souders, p. 11 bottom/ William Whitehurst, p. 9 left; Pauline Cottrill, p. 9 right; Getty Images/ PhotoDisc, pp. 10 bottom, 27 centre/ Stone, p. 22 left/ Taxi, pp. 16 left, 27 bottom; Image Addict, pp. 25 left, 27 top; National Institute of Standards and Technology, USA, p. 23 right; National Maritime Museum Greenwich/ Photo Studio/ Lisa MacLeod, p. 26; Photolibrary.com/ Bridgeman Art Library, p. 19/ James Gual, pp. 8-9/ Science Photo Library/Adam Hart-Davis, p. 11 top; The Picture Source/ Terry Oakley, p. 16 right; Science and Society Picture Library, pp. 15, 22 right, 24, 25 right.

PM Plus Non Fiction
Sapphire
Colour Around Us
The Science of Cooking
Fibres in Fashion
Making Shapes
Built Like That
Measure for Measure

ISBN 978 0 17 009942 4
ISBN 978 0 17 009939 4 (set)

Cengage Learning Australia
Level 5, 80 Dorcas Street
Southbank VIC 3006 Australia
Phone: 1300 790 853
Email: aust.nelsonprimary@cengage.com

For learning solutions, visit **cengage.com.au**

Printed in China by 1010 Printing International Ltd
4 5 6 7 8 9 10 13 12 11 10 09

Contents

Introduction

Your family is going on a holiday. After four hours of driving, you're still chugging along in the car.

'Are we there yet?' you call out.

'It shouldn't be much longer,' your mother says.

You gaze out the window. 'I wonder how tall those gum trees are.'

'And how far away would that mountain peak be?' asks your father, unfolding a road map.

The car passes a huge boulder on the side of the road. 'That's a gigantic rock!' your sister remarks. 'I wonder what it weighs.'

The car zooms across a bridge. 'How fast are we going?' you ask.

'Guess!' your mother says.

'Ninety kilometres an hour?'

'Close,' your mother replies, as she looks at the car's speedometer. 'We're going 95 kilometres an hour.'

'What time is it?' your sister asks.

'Guess!' your father replies.

Your sister looks outside at the shadows of trees. 'I think it's four o'clock,' she announces.

Your father looks at his watch. 'Not bad. It's half-past four. We're getting close to the national park now.'

'What direction is the park from here?' you ask.

Your father studies the map. 'We go north a few kilometres, and then turn west into the park.'

At the top of a hill, your mother parks the car. Everyone gets out and gazes at a deep green valley below, and the snow-topped mountains in the distance.

Your father looks at the gathering clouds. 'We'd better get going. It looks like a storm is coming.'

'How do you know?' you ask.

'All these questions!' your father says. 'How tall are the trees? How far away is that mountain? How much does that rock weigh? How fast are we going? What time is it? What direction is the park? Is there a storm coming?'

You laugh. 'I guess we're just curious!'

'It's a good thing we have the technology these days to help us answer those questions,' says your mother.

You lean back in the seat and think. How did people long ago figure out the answer to those questions? What kinds of instruments do people use today? Who invented them?

Read on, and find out!

Chapter 1

Distance

How far away is that mountain? How tall is that tree? These are questions about distance. Distance is the amount of space between one place and another.

In ancient times

Long ago, people used their own bodies – arms, hands, fingers and feet — as the **units of measure** for distance.

The most common unit was the foot. To measure the distance of a path, someone walked heel-to-toe along it and counted each time they set down a foot. If they set down their feet 20 times, the path was 20 feet long.

However, there was a problem with using bodies as units of measure. People are not all the same size, so the units were not always the same. People with smaller feet would measure distances differently than people with larger feet.

Historical measures

Unit	Original measure	Measure today
Finger (digit)	Width of a finger	1.91 cm
Inch, unch or uncia	Width of the thumb. Later, three grains of barley placed end to end.	2.54 cm
Hand	Distance across the width of a hand. Also, four fingers.	10.16 cm
Span	Distance between the tip of the thumb and the tip of the little finger with the hand stretched out	22.86 cm
Cubit	Distance from the elbow to the tip of the middle finger (cubitum is Latin for 'elbow')	50.8 cm
Yard	Length of a particular type of belt. Later, the distance from the chin or nose to the tips of the fingers.	90 cm
Foot	Length of adult male's foot	30.48 cm
Pace	Distance of two regular walking steps	1.8 m
Rod	Length of 16 men's feet put heel to toe	4.95 m
Furlong	40 rods long, or the length of a furrow made by a plough on a farm	198 m
Mile	1 000 paces	1 584 m

Standard measures

As civilisations grew and people started settling other lands, they wanted the units of measure to be the same for everyone. To do this, they needed to agree on a length for each unit. Once a specific length was set, a **standard** was made.

The imperial, or English, system of measurement includes many of the ancient units of measure based on the body, such as inches, feet and miles. The United States still uses the imperial system.

*In 1592, the length of Queen Elizabeth's arm became the official **yard.***

The metric system

In 1791, the French created a new way of measuring called the metric system. The word 'metric' is Greek for 'measure'. The metric system is based on units of 10. All the units are related to each other. This makes it easy for people to change from one metric unit to another.

At first, many French people did not use the metric system because they were not used to it. However, in 1840, France made a law that required everyone to use it. Over the next hundred years, most countries switched to the metric system.

Metric units of measure for distance

Unit	Value
Kilometre (km)	1 000 metres
Hectometre (hm)	100 metres
Decametre (dam)	10 metres
Metre (m)	1 metre
Decimetre (dm)	0.1 metre or 1/10 metre
Centimetre (cm)	0.01 metre or 1/100 metre
Millimetre (mm)	0.001 metre or 1/1000 metre

Odometers are instruments that measure distance. In the past, odometers were run by gears that moved a counting device. Today, odometers measure distance using a small computer.

Speed

Distance is often measured in speed, which is how fast something travels from one place to another. In the 1800s, steam engines established the first speed record at 46.69 kilometres an hour. In the early 1900s, aeroplanes travelled about 48 kilometres an hour. Today's aeroplanes travel at speeds of up to 1 207 kilometres an hour. ***Supersonic*** *planes can travel faster than the* ***speed of sound****, which is more than 1 191 kilometres an hour.*

Direction

Direction is the way that something is moving or pointing. The main directions are north, south, east and west. People use a compass to find north. From that, they can determine the other directions.

Radar guns are used by police to measure the speed of cars. The radar gun gives out **radio waves** that bounce off the moving car. The length of these waves changes as the car moves past. The gun measures the waves and determines the speed of the car. Radar guns are also used to measure the speed of balls in sports such as tennis, hockey, baseball and soccer.

Ship speed

Sailors use a measure called a knot to measure distances and speed. A knot equals one **nautical mile** an hour. If a ship is travelling at 10 knots, its speed is 18.52 kilometres an hour.

In ancient times, sailors used a knotmeter to determine their sailing speed in knots. A knotmeter was a rope with knots tied every 7.71 metres along the rope. A sailor threw the knotmeter overboard, and the speed of the ship was determined by how many knots went out during a certain period of time.

Today, a ship's speed is measured with **ultra-sonic** instruments that use sound waves to measure the movement of the boat.

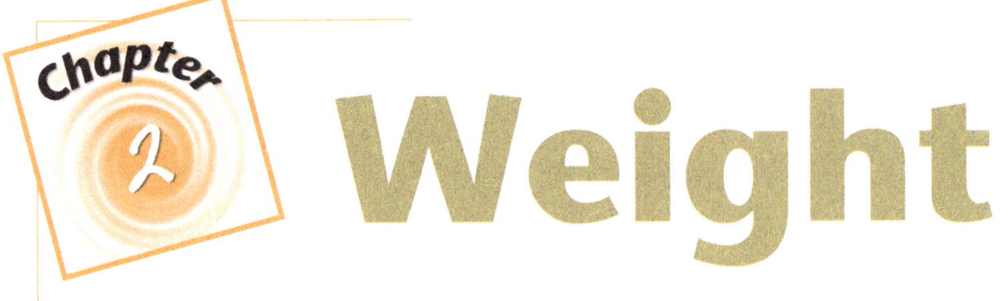

Chapter 2 Weight

How much does that rock weigh? The weight of something is how heavy it is. Objects have weight because of gravity. Gravity is the force that pulls objects down toward the Earth's centre. When someone steps on a scale, gravity pulls them downward. If they weigh 40 kilograms, gravity pulls them down with that same force of 40 kilograms.

Astronauts in space float because there is no gravity in space. This means there is no force pulling down on them.

The farther away an object is from the centre of the Earth — or any massive body — the less the object weighs. If people were able to weigh themselves on other planets, their weight would vary. They would weigh more on larger planets than on smaller planets.

Weight of a person on the Moon and on planets

Planet	Kilograms
Earth	74
Earth's Moon	12
Mercury	28
Venus	67
Mars	28
Jupiter	175
Saturn	68
Uranus	66
Neptune	84
Pluto	5

In ancient times

Long ago, people did not understand weight. They measured things by how many objects they could carry. For example, a person could carry a bundle of straw, or six rocks. However, this did not tell how much something weighed.

Later, people started comparing the weight of objects. They would hold both objects in their hands and feel which one was heaviest.

In 5000 BC, the Egyptians developed a simple stickscale that measured which object was heavier. They hung a stick by a cord, and then tied an object to each end of the stick. The object that weighed the most pulled its end of the stick downward. If the objects weighed the same, the stick stayed parallel to the ground.

Around 3000 BC, the Egyptians made weights from different-sized stones. They hung pans on the stick scale and placed the stones in one pan. In the other pan they placed the object they wanted to weigh. They measured the weight of the object by how many stones were needed to balance the scale.

Later, these stone weights were standardised. This meant that everyone used weights of the same size and **density.** Food, money, metals and medicine were measured using stone weights.

An old-fashioned scale with a collection of standardised weights.

Modern weights

Today, people can weigh themselves on simple household scales. Larger objects, such as elephants and heavy trucks, are weighed on special scales. These scales work just like household scales, except they are much bigger.

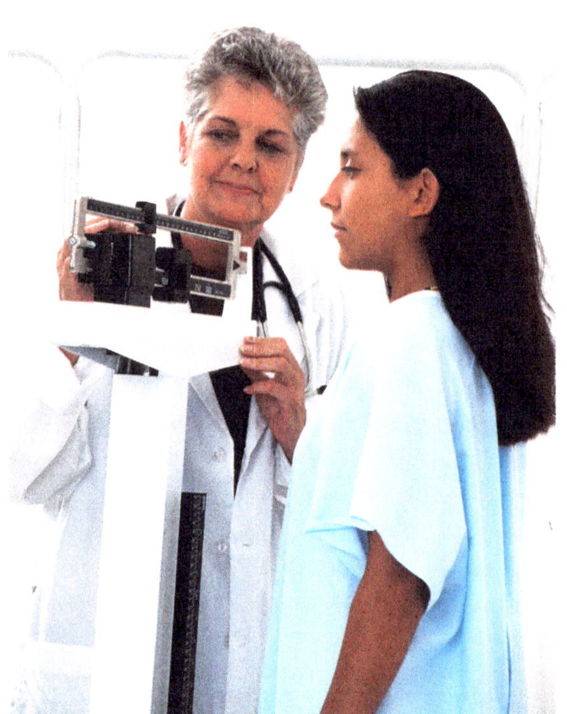

Doctors' offices have very accurate scales.

Cars are weighed on a weighbridge.

People often wonder about the weight of Balanced Rock at Arches National Park in the United States. Perched on a pillar of rock, Balanced Rock is estimated to weigh about three million kilograms. Geologists could not actually weigh the rock, so they estimated its weight. They took a sample of the rock and measured and weighed it. Then they multiplied that weight by the total size of the rock to get the estimated weight.

Time

How long have we been driving? When will we have lunch? These are questions about time. Time is a measure of the past, present and future. People keep track of time with calendars and clocks.

Units of time

second	1/60 of a minute
minute	60 seconds or 1/60 of an hour
hour	60 minutes or 1/24 of a day
day	24 hours – the time it takes for the Earth to rotate once on its axis
week	Seven days or about 1/4 of a month
month	About 30 days, or 1/12 of a year – the time it takes for the Moon to travel around the Earth
season	Spring, summer, autumn and winter – each season is about 90 days long, or 1/4 of a year
year	365.25 days – the time it takes the Earth to travel around the Sun
decade	10 years
century	100 years
millennium	1 000 years

Calendars

A calendar measures time in years, months, weeks and days. Our calendar was developed over thousands of years.

In ancient times, people kept track of time by watching the regular patterns of the Sun and Moon. They scratched lines into calendar sticks made of wood or bone to mark the passing days, months and years.

An ancient calendar stick

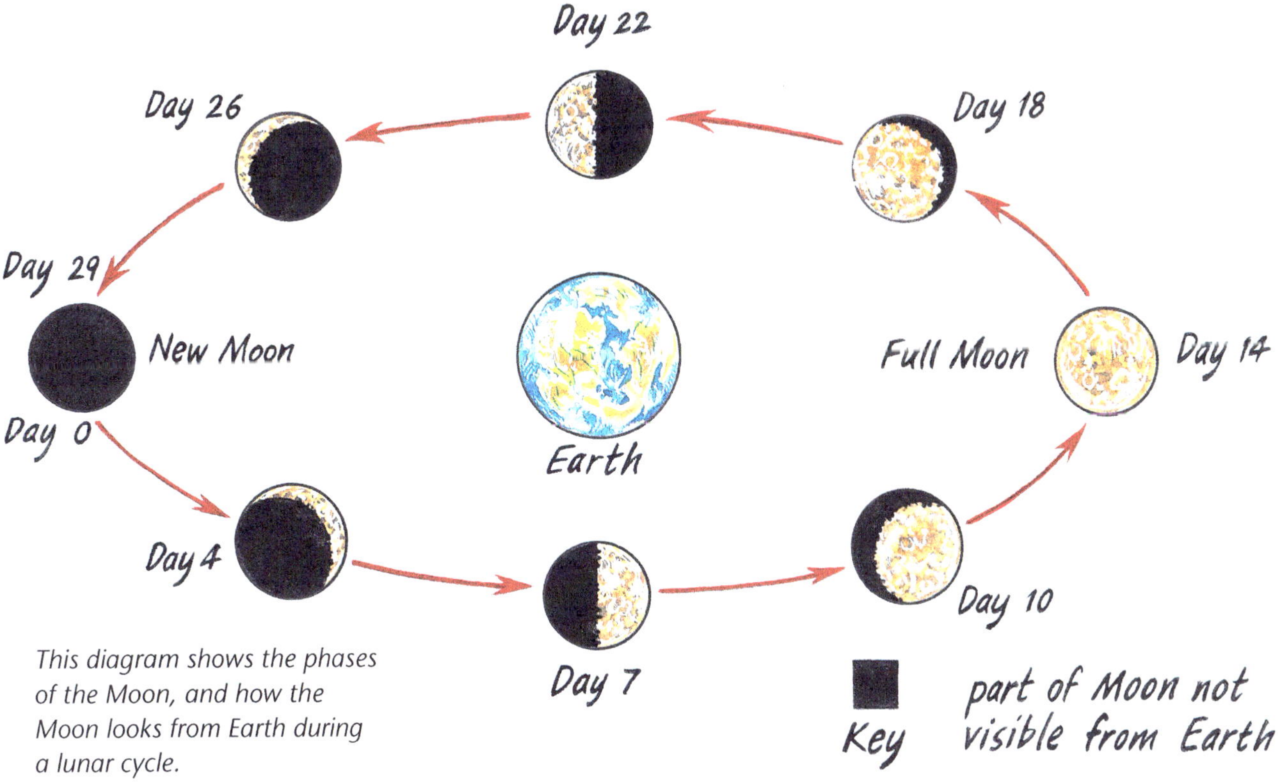

About 5000 years ago, people started creating lunar calendars, which are based on the phases of the Moon. Every 29.53 days (about one month), the Moon travels all the way around the Earth. Twelve of these cycles make a lunar year, which is 354.36 days. A calendar based on the lunar year is called a lunar calendar. The Babylonians, Chinese, Greeks, Romans and Egyptians used lunar calendars.

Day 22

Day 26

Day 18

Day 29

New Moon

Earth

Full Moon

Day 14

Day 0

Day 4

Day 7

Day 10

Key part of Moon not visible from Earth

This diagram shows the phases of the Moon, and how the Moon looks from Earth during a lunar cycle.

The Mayans — and later, the Egyptians — developed a solar calendar based on the Earth's movement around the Sun. A solar calendar is based on the solar year, which is the time it takes for the Earth to travel all the way around the Sun. A solar year is 365.25 days, or 365 days and six hours long.

In 45 BC, the Romans started using a solar calendar. The solar year is a few hours longer than 365 days, so the Romans added an extra day every four years to create a 'leap year'. They called this the Julian calendar, after Julius Caesar, a Roman ruler. In 1582, Pope Gregory XIII made this calendar more accurate. Most of the world still uses the Gregorian calendar today.

Days of the week

The ancient Romans named the days after Roman gods, and the **Anglo-Saxons** had their own names. Our names for the days of the week are taken from Anglo-Saxon names.

Day	What named for	Roman	Anglo-Saxon	Modern names
1	Sun	Sol	Sun	Sunday
2	Moon	Luna	Moon	Monday
3	Mars	Mars	Tiw	Tuesday
4	Mercury	Mercury	Woden	Wednesday
5	Jupiter	Jupiter	Thor	Thursday
6	Venus	Venus	Frigg	Friday
7	Saturn	Saturn	Saturn	Saturday

Months of the year

In 27 BC, the Roman calendar had 12 months:

Januarius			
Februarius	Aprilis	Julius	October
Martius	Maius	Augustus	November
	Junius	[illegible]	[illegible]

Our months are still named after these Roman months.

Clocks

Time is also measured in smaller units called hours, minutes and seconds. People use clocks to measure these units.

Long ago, people used shadow sticks to keep track of time. They placed a stick straight up in the ground. As the sun moved across the sky, the stick's shadow moved in an arc around the stick. People looked at the shadow during daylight and knew the approximate time of day.

The sundial uses shadows to tell the time. A sundial has a circular dial with the hours marked on it and a triangular pointer in the middle. People told time by seeing where the pointer's shadow fell on the hour marks.

About 325 BC, the ancient Egyptians built water clocks. Water dripped from an upper container into a lower container. Marks inside the lower container showed how much time had passed.

People also measured time using candle clocks and hourglasses. As a candle clock burns, markings down the side of the candle measure the passing time. In an hourglass, sand falling from one glass to another one shows how much time has gone by.

An hourglass

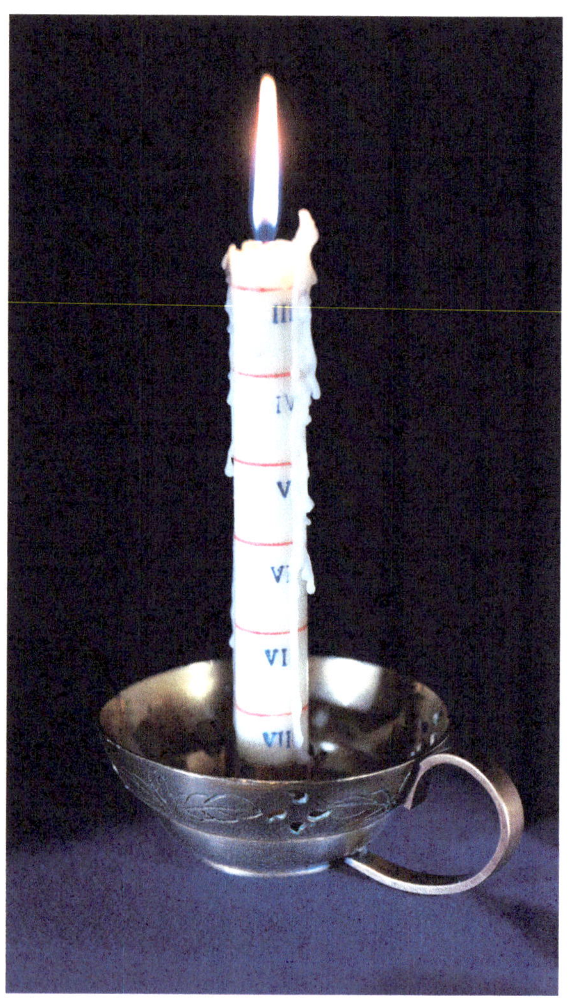

A candle clock

In the 1300s, a mechanical clock was invented. This type of clock contains a weight that is pulled down by gravity and spins gears that move the clock's hands. In the 1400s, springs replaced the weights.

A mechanical clock

A pendulum clock

In 1656, a Dutch scientist named Christian Huygens built a pendulum clock. A pendulum swings in a steady motion, which keeps the hands turning at an even rate.

In 1929, an American scientist named Warren A. Marrison designed a quartz clock. Quartz is a **crystal** that vibrates when electricity flows through it. This keeps the hands of the clock moving at a steady rate.

In 1949, an **atomic** clock was invented. Atomic clocks are so accurate that since the 1960s, they have been used to keep the official time for the world. Scientists continue to build more accurate versions of the atomic clock. The latest one loses only about one second in 20 million years.

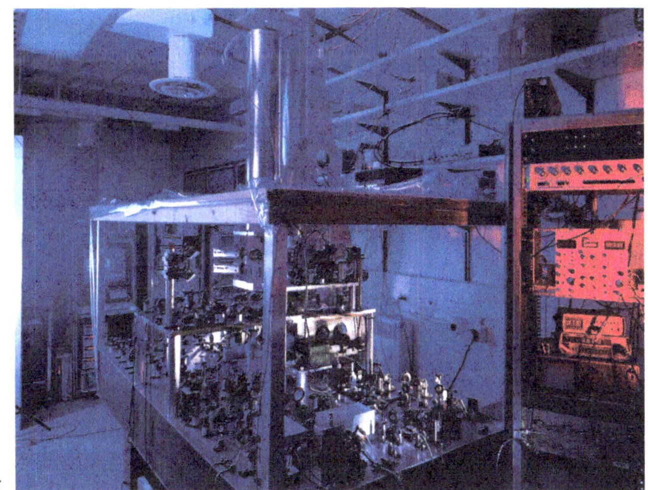
An atomic clock

Chapter 4

Weather

Weather is the condition of the air outside. The weather might be hot or cold, calm or windy, clear or rainy. Temperature, air pressure and wind are some of the weather conditions that can be measured.

Temperature

Temperature is a measure of how much heat there is. The more heat, the warmer the temperature is; the less heat, the cooler it is.

Thermometers are used to measure temperature. The first one was invented in 1593 by Galileo Galilei. In this device, tiny glass globes floated inside a cylinder filled with liquid. On warmer days, the liquid became less dense and the globes dropped down. On cooler days, the liquid became denser and the globes floated upward.

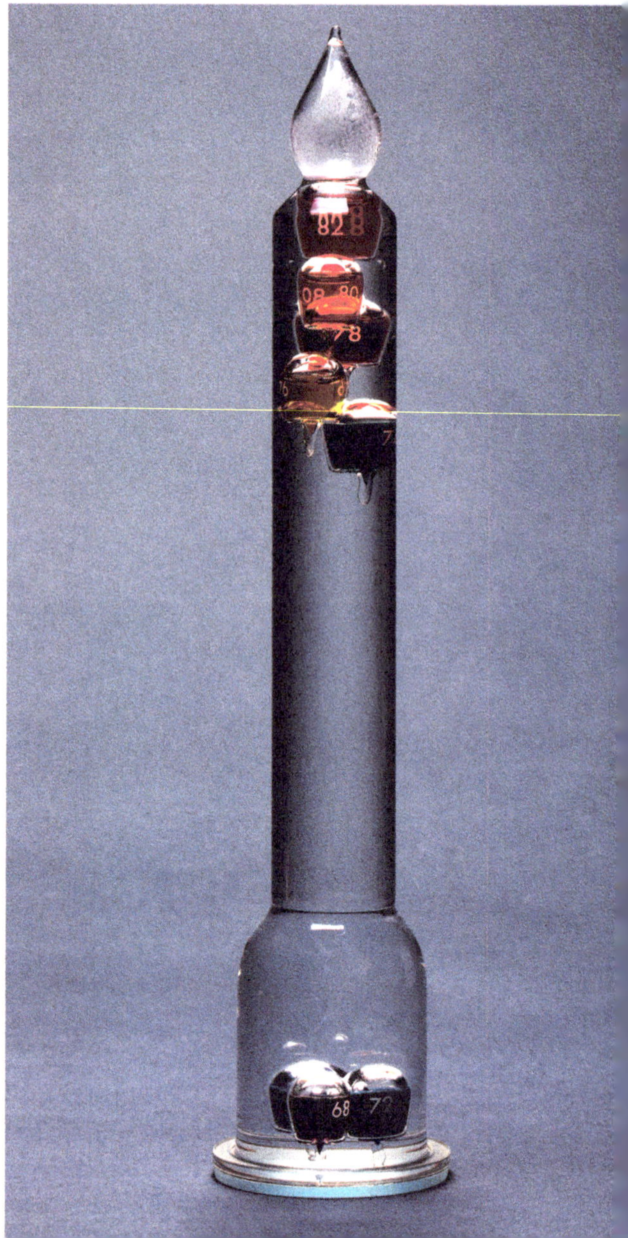

A Galileo thermometer

In 1714, Gabriel Fahrenheit invented the **mercury** thermometer. In this thermometer, the mercury expanded up the tube when it was warm, and dropped back down when it was cold. The mercury thermometer is still used today.

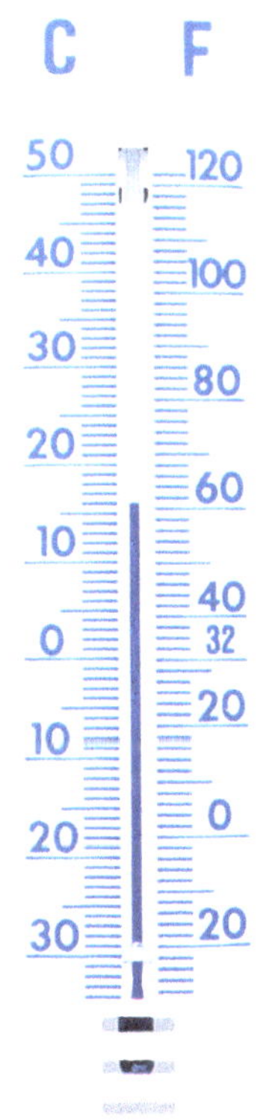

An early mercury thermometer (above) and a modern one (left).

Comparison of Fahrenheit and Celsius temperature scales

	Fahrenheit	Celsius
Boiling point	212°F	100°C
Freezing point	32°F	0°C

Air pressure

Air pressure is the weight of the **atmosphere** in a certain location. Low pressure is created when warm air starts rising. When the warm air has risen, it cools and forms clouds, which usually means a storm is coming.

High pressure occurs when cool air sinks and warms near the surface of the Earth. High pressure usually means fine weather.

Air pressure is measured with a barometer. In 1644, Evangelista Torricelli invented the first barometer. He set the end of a long tube in a bowl of mercury. When there was high pressure it pushed down on the mercury in the bowl, forcing it up the tube. When there was low pressure, the mercury in the tube dropped down. Later, a scale was added to the tube so the air pressure could be measured.

A thunder glass or storm glass is a barometer that uses water instead of mercury. A glass globe with a spout is filled with water. High pressure pushes down on the water in the spout, causing it to drop. Water rises up the spout when there is low pressure. These barometers were often used on small ships in the 1800s so sailors could tell when a storm was coming.

A storm glass

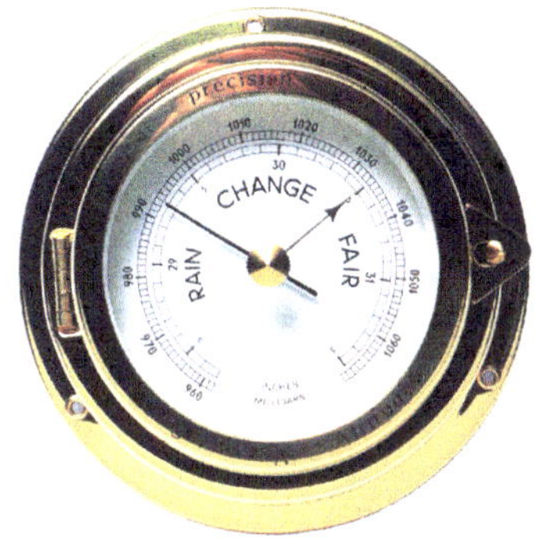

An aneroid barometer

Modern barometers come in several forms. The aneroid barometer is the most commonly used household barometer. It does not use liquid. Instead, it contains a box with no air in it. When there is high pressure, the sides of the box squeeze inward and cause the pointer on the dial to move one way. Low pressure makes the sides of the box expand, moving the pointer in the other direction.

Wind

A wind sock

Wind is created when air moves from an area of high pressure to an area of low pressure.

If people know which direction the wind is blowing, they can often figure out what type of weather is coming. Wind vanes and wind socks indicate wind direction. A wind vane twirls on a post, and an arrow on it points in the direction the wind is blowing from. A wind sock shows the direction the wind is heading. One end is tied to a post, and the loose end is carried outward by the wind.

A wind vane

In the past, people measured wind speed with the Beaufort Wind Scale. To use this scale, people looked at how the wind was affecting trees or other objects outside. Then they compared what they saw to the descriptions on the wind scale. Sir Francis Beaufort, a British Admiral, invented this scale in 1805 for sailors. It was later adapted for land use.

The Beaufort Wind Scale, adapted for use on land

Beaufort Wind Scale

Beaufort number	Wind speed (km/hour)	Description	Effect
0	under 1	Calm	Smoke rises vertically
1	1-5	Light air	Smoke drifts
2	6-11	Light breeze	Leaves rustle
3	12-19	Gentle breeze	Leaves and twigs move
4	20-28	Moderate breeze	Small branches move
5	29-38	Fresh breeze	Small trees move
6	39-49	Strong breeze	Large branches move
7	50-61	Near gale	Whole trees move
8	62-74	Gale	Twigs break
9	75-88	Strong gale	Branches break
10	89-102	Storm	Trees uprooted
11	103-117	Violent storm	Widespread damage
12	118 +	Cyclone	Extreme damage

Today, people measure the speed of the wind with an anemometer. One type of anemometer has several cups that spin around a post as they catch the wind. An electric meter attached to this device measures the speed of the spinning cups.

An anemometer

Tornadoes are powerful, spinning windstorms that can occur during large thunderstorms. The Fujita Scale measures the strength of tornadoes according to the force of the wind, the distance the tornado travelled on the ground, and how much damage it caused.

Conclusion

'That was a great trip, wasn't it?' your father says, as the car drives south on the highway.

'Except for all that wind and rain,' your mother says, shaking her head.

'And that hike was so long!' you add.

'But wasn't it worth it to see the long, winding rivers and the deep, green valleys surrounded by the tall, snowy mountains?' your mother asks.

'Yes!' you and your sister say together.

'Maybe we'll come back next year.'

'That's a good idea,' your father says, 'since we didn't have enough time to see everything. Next year, I'll bring my watch so we can keep better track of time.'

'We should bring scales, too, so we can weigh our backpacks!' your sister says.

You laugh. 'How about a tape measure to see how far we hiked?'

'And weather instruments,' your mother adds. 'So the wind and the rain won't catch us by surprise!'

'Maybe you should start reading instruments now Dad!' you exclaim. 'You're going over the speed limit!'

Your father looks at the speedometer and slows the car down. 'Well, that's one measuring device we did bring!'

Glossary

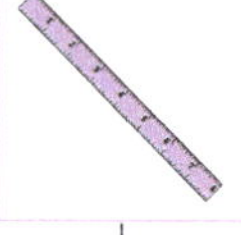

Anglo-Saxons	the people of ancient England
atmosphere	the gases that surround Earth
atomic	using energy from atoms
crystal	a type of rock
density	how heavy or light an object is for its size
mercury	a silvery-white liquid metallic element
nautical mile	a unit of distance used mostly by sailors; approximately 1 852 metres
radio waves	invisible waves of electromagnetic energy that exist all around us
speed of sound	how fast sound travels; approximately 1 191 kilometres an hour
standard	a model for all other measuring devices
supersonic	faster than the speed of sound
ultrasonic	using sound waves that are beyond what humans can hear
unit of measure	a given size, weight or value used in measuring; a metre is an example of a unit of measure
yard	an imperial unit of measure equivalent to one metre